Naughty Jackie

AF673789

Om KIDZ
An imprint of Om Books International

First Published in 2023

Om Kidz | Om Books International

Corporate & Editorial Office
A-12, Sector 64, Noida 201 301
Uttar Pradesh, India
Phone: +91 120 477 4100
Email: editorial@ombooks.com
Website: www.ombooksinternational.com

Sales Office
107, Ansari Road, Darya Ganj
New Delhi 110 002, India
Phone: +91 11 4000 9000
Email: sales@ombooks.com

ISBN: 978-93-94547-22-3

Printed in India

10 9 8 7 6 5 4 3 2 1

Naughty Jackie

I'm all set to read

Paste your photograph here

My name is

Jackie, a white **puppy**,
lived **with** John's
grandfather.
Jackie was two months
old **when** grandfather
brought him **home**.

Jackie was now almost six months old. He had become a **very** naughty pup!

NEWS
WORLD NEWS TODAY

One morning, **grandfather** sat in the garden **reading** the morning **newspaper**. He took off his **shoes** to relax.

Jackie **crept** up silently and ran off **with them! Grandfather** didn't notice!
When he looked **down** to wear his **shoes**, **they** were gone!
He understood who had taken the **shoes**. He **laughed**. He knew that Jackie would soon bring **them** back.

Grandfather and Jackie **would** go for a walk **every** evening. Jackie **would** run after the colourful butterflies, **barking** loudly.

He **chased** rabbits too. But he **never** strayed far **away from grandfather**.

One day, **grandfather** and Jackie **went** for a walk in the evening. Suddenly it started **raining** heavily.

Grandfather was caught by surprise. He wasn’t carrying an umbrella.

Jackie got drenched within a minute. He began to **shake** himself wildly, **splashing grandfather** even **more**.

Both of **them**
ran as fast as
they could.
They stood under
a big willow **tree**.
Rain was pouring hard.
As **they** waited, lightning
lit up the sky.

"Let's move **away from** the **trees**, Jackie. It's not safe to hide here **when** lightning takes place."

BANG! The lightning hit a **tree**. Jackie and **grandfather** started **running away from** the **tree very** fast

They saw a **shed** in the distance.
"Let's hide in **that shed**."
Jackie pushed the **door** open
with his paw.
They went inside.

It was finally nice and dry. **There were** old foldable **chairs** inside. **Grandfather** sank down **into** one of **them**.

“A great and safe place to stay till the rain stops,” he **said** and smiled.

But Jackie started **growling** loudly. **Grandfather** looked at him, puzzled. "What's up, boy?"

Then, over in a corner, he saw two pairs of glowing **eyes**. **They moved very** close to the back of **grandfather's chair**.

And forward **jumped** an angry and **very** hungry fox. He **rushed** towards them, but Jackie charged at the fox. Even though he was small, he **jumped** onto the fox's neck.

He bit it as hard as he **could**.

The fox let out a howl. He ran out of the shed to save himself. **Grandfather** got out of the **chair** and picked up Jackie, holding him tenderly in his arms. “You saved my life, Jackie boy. I am going to give you an extra large bone to chew on.” Jackie was happy and barked with joy.

Know Your Words

Sight Words

away	into	then	went
could	more	them	were
down	never	there	when
every	said	they	with
from	that	very	would

Naming Words

chairs	home	shoes
door	newspaper	tree
eyes	puppy	
grandfather	shed	

Doing Words

barked	growling	reading
barking	jumped	running
buzzing	moved	rushed
chased	picked	shake
crept	raining	splashing